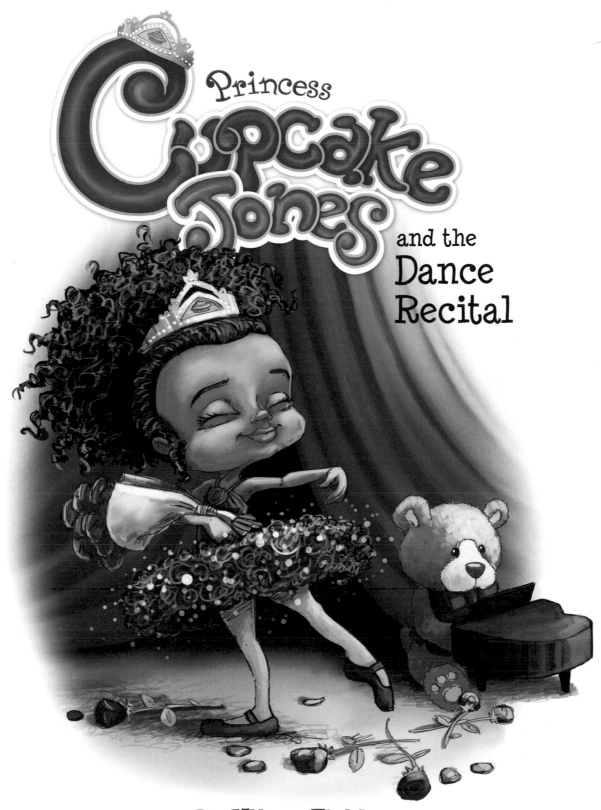

Princess Cupcake Jones

and the
Dance Recital

By Ylleya Fields

Illustrated by Michael LaDuca

Belle Publishing · Cleveland, Ohio

To all of our Cupcakettes: We love you all so much! Thanks for continuing to support everything we do. A special thank you to our JCD family. Without you this book would never have been written!

Belle Publishing
5247 Wilson Mills Rd #324
Cleveland OH 44143
www.BellePublishing.net

Book design and illustrations by Michael LaDuca, Luminus Media LLC

ISBN: 978-0-9909986-7-9

Publisher's Cataloging-In-Publication Data
(Prepared by The Donohue Group, Inc.)

Names: Fields, Ylleya. | LaDuca, Michael, illustrator.
Title: Princess Cupcake Jones and the dance recital / by Ylleya Fields ;
    illustrated by Michael LaDuca.

Other Titles: Cupcake Jones and the dance recital
Description: Cleveland, Ohio : Belle Publishing, [2016] | Series:
    [Princess Cupcake Jones series] ; [4] | Interest age level: 004-008. |
    Summary: Princess Cupcake Jones loves taking dance classes at Madame's
    School of Ballet. However, there's one move that Cupcake can't quite
    do-- an arabesque. While all of her friends are excited about the dance
    recital, Cupcake is nervous that she won't be able to do it. Follow
    Princess Cupcake Jones as she learns that with practice and
    determination there isn't anything she can't do if she puts her mind to
    it.
Identifiers: ISBN 978-0-9909986-7-9
Subjects: LCSH: Princesses--Juvenile fiction. | Dance recitals--Juvenile
    fiction. | Determination (Personality trait)--Juvenile fiction. |
    Stories in rhyme. | CYAC: Princesses--Fiction. | Dance recitals--
    Fiction. | Determination (Personality trait)--Fiction.
Classification: LCC PZ7.F545 Prd 2015 | DDC [Fic]--dc23

Princess Cupcake liked to paint and sing
but dancing was her favorite thing.
She'd pose in the park and spin in the sun.
Playing prima ballerina was so much fun!

Cupcake loved Madame's School of Ballet.
She attended with Violet, Jane, and Soleil.

They practiced their twirls, their jumps, and leaps,
their pliés and jetés 'til pink in the cheeks.

Madame was strict, though always fair.
"Your backs must be as straight as a chair!
No lateness, gum, or tights with holes!
A leotard must fit. No saggy rolls!"

"She makes us do homework!" Jane said in a huff.
"Whew!" said Soleil. "Ballet sure is tough!"
Cupcake tried hard not to grumble like some.
Plus, her homework was always, yes, ALWAYS was done.

Yet, there was one thing Cupcake couldn't master.
Her arabesque was a dancing disaster!
She tried her best to stand on one shoe,
but that was a trick her foot wouldn't do.

She made up excuses. For instance, she'd say.
"Madame, I can't! I have a blister today."

"Next week at recital that leg must be straight!
Your nose pointed up, you must elevate!"

Had she not paid attention? Was the recital so soon?
Her friends didn't worry. They were over the moon!

When class was over, Jane shouted with glee.
"I can't wait to see what our costumes will be!
I hope they're purple or pink is good too!"
Soleil turned to Cupcake, "Well... what about you?"

"It doesn't matter," she said with a frown.
She trudged toward home with her head down.

"What's wrong?" asked the Queen. "You seem a bit blue.
Is the dance recital worrying you?"

"I can't arabesque," Cupcake said with a pout.
"Oh," said the Queen. "That's what this is about?
As long as you try and do your best,
everyone watching will be so impressed."

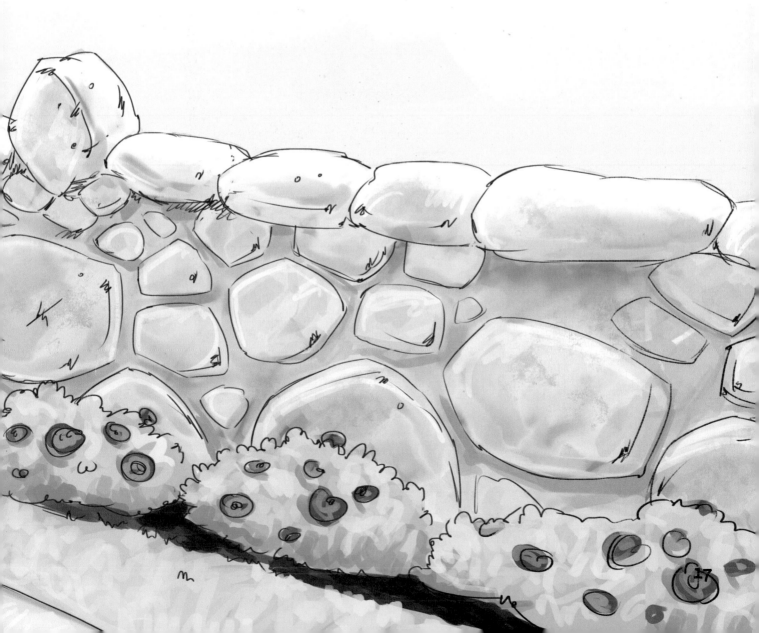

All that week, Cupcake practiced with flair.
She lifted her leg up high in the air.

18

She practiced and practiced across every floor.
At school and at home, 'til each toe was sore.

19

At the recital, Cupcake Jones wasn't scared.
With all of her practice, she felt more than prepared.

While she was excited, her friends were not ready.
Violet was shivering. Soleil looked unsteady.

"We can't do it!" Jane said. "We're all a big mess!"
"Don't worry," said Cupcake, while they all got dressed.

"My mom says to give it our best, and she's right!
There's no need for jitters, tears, or stage fright."

"Are you ready?" asked Madame. They stood in a line.
"On stage now girls. It's your time to shine!"

Every parent sat perched on the edge of their seat.
The music began. The girls danced to the beat.
With each move the girls made, their confidence grew.
As they did their arabesques, the crowd whispered, "Ooooh!"

Cupcake had done the best that she could.
And backstage, Madame said, "You did really good!"

The girls heard their parents cheer loud from the crowd.
The King was the loudest. "I've never been more proud!"

After the show he scooped Cupcake into the air.
"Can you show me that move that you did up there?"

"Of course, Dad." Cupcake smiled. "As you command."
Cupcake and her parents danced off hand in hand.

MADAME'S SCHOOL OF BALLET